The worst part of the end of the world is the terrible silence…

Silence was one of the hardest things to get used to. I had always had background noise around me: the sounds of cars or airplanes, the constant hum of electricity. The quiet was deafening. Luckily I had Grant and now we had the others. The sounds of their movements helped to ease the feeling that I was completely alone.

Gone were the tall majestic evergreens and the dense forest floor covered with fern and salal. Before, the forest had been a place where there was rich spongy soil underfoot and you heard the constant bubbling of ice-cold streams and the piney taste of cool forest air was thick on the tongue and face.

Now everything was dead and dry.

THE
RECKONING

Edited by R. Edgewood

Published by 53rd Street Publishing
Offices in Gibsons, B.C. Canada and Lincoln City,
Oregon

The Reckoning

Published by 53rd Street Publishing
Copyright 2015 53rd street publishing

Cover art © Can Stock Photo Inc. / rolffimages
Print ISBN 978-1-927621-47-9
Edited by Colleen Kuehne
Cover designed by R. Edgewood
Cover design and layout © 2015 by 53rd Street
Publishing

53rd Street Publishing
Head office: Gibsons B.C. Canada
www.53rdstreetpublishing.com

Collections from 53rd Street Publishing

Ladies of the Jolly Roger
Nightmares
The Reckoning

Contents

Forward

Creating a collection for authors is like raising a child. You need a lot of input and a lot of help.

The first thing you have to do is decide on a theme for the stories. These days end of the world or apocalypse stories seem all the rage so we decided the time was right for 53rd Street Publishing to put together our own take on doomsday.

We searched our inventory and lo and behold we found some excellent stories by two talented authors. After gaining their agreement to participate in the collection you hold in your hands (or are seeing on your e-reader screen) we are providing these stories for you the reader to enjoy.

So sit back and enjoy the end of the world as we at 53rd Street Publishing see it. This is our child.

R. Edgewood
Editor

Introduction

The end of the world has been depicted on film and in books since time began. The Bible has an entire book devoted to the end of the world.

On television popular shows such as Z Nation and The Walking Dead explore the zombie apocalypse.

Theatrical films such as A Boy and His Dog (derived from the story by the legendary Harlan Ellison), Escape from New York, and On The Beach have fostered a possible dark future ahead.

The authors in this collection explore the humanity behind the end of the world. Will we go down fighting or with a whimper? Do we have a choice?

These and other questions are explored in these stories and we have selected them for this very purpose.

R. Edgewood
Series Editor
November 2015

Neighborhood Watch

THE FLICKERING FLAME from the oil lamp cast twisted, writhing shadows over the walls of Pete Simpson's recreation room in the basement of his split-level, four-bedroom house. The large room was a real man cave. Even after all this time, the room still smelled of cigar smoke and beer, though we hadn't had either of those luxuries since this all began six weeks ago. We four neighborhood watch members were seated around a seven-player mahogany poker table. The playing surface was covered in a tobacco-colored leather, with integrated chip wells and cup holders. We were waiting for the arrival of the fifth member of our group. Seven armless, matching leather chairs surrounded the table.

Only we weren't here to play poker.

Along the walls of the oblong-shaped room were burnished steel shelves containing trophies and plaques from Pete's days as a high school and state collegiate athlete. Amongst these personal treasures were his sports collectibles signed baseballs, basketballs, and footballs representing every pro team in the state of Washington and in Portland, Oregon, just across the Columbia River.

In a wide gap in the bookshelves was a sixty-inch flat screen television. Facing the large digital TV were two rows of leather recliners, five chairs in each row. The simulated oak flooring stood up to the punishment of Sunday NFL games and final four weekends.

Pete hadn't been a star amongst his athletic peers but he had been pretty good. Too bad for him, others were better. They received the scholarships while Pete became a used car salesman who lived in our middle class neighborhood on the outskirts of Vancouver. He was trapped in suburbia along with the rest of us.

Of course, his collectibles and trophies were worthless now. No one is going to barter for a can of tuna with a collectible anymore, not when cash money, gold, and diamonds have no value.

Especially when you and your family will starve to death without food. Food and water meant survival. How ironic it was that we'd wasted our lives striving for now worthless *stuff*.

"Where's Oscar?" asked Alice, who was seated across from me, her dark eyes narrowed to slits. She was constantly wringing her hands as if washing them. Her short brown hair was oily and she reeked of sour sweat, but then, didn't we all? None of us had had enough water to shower or bathe for weeks now. We'd thought about going to the river, but being outside our barricaded neighborhood was risky and presented serious security issues for us.

My poor friend, Alice, was nervous and becoming increasingly edgy over the past few days. Recent events had brought us all to the edge of our sanity.

The lacquered pine paneling that lined the walls behind the shelves had always bothered me. Who in their right mind would keep this cheap '60s crap on their walls? I rolled my eyes since I knew the answer without asking the question. A Neanderthal like Pete, seated to my right, of course. With his thinning hair and receding hairline and expanding beer gut, he had become the poster boy around the neighborhood for the fading athlete.

Now, of course, he was a shriveled man—half his former size, with sunken, grizzled cheeks.

"Got the time?" I asked Conrad, seated across the table from me. He looked at his mechanical watch and his lips formed a grim, humorless line. "He's more than an hour overdue."

I slapped Pete's left shoulder with the back of my hand. "I thought you said he'd be back with the scouting party by now?"

Pete scowled at me, his piercing cobalt eyes angry. "Knock it off, Liz, I'm as worried about them as you are. We *all* know the risks."

"Yeah," I said, sweeping stray lengths of my scraggly, dirty-blonde hair away from over my eyes with my arm. I hadn't had a decent haircut in weeks and had decided earlier today to shave my head completely as many of the neighborhood women and some men had done, although I loved my long hair. It had taken years to grow it this long.

"But they promised us we had ninety days," said May. "Surely we can last at least that long." May was Chinese-American, with dark, almond-shaped eyes that seemed to look right through you, and high cheekbones. She'd always been thin but now her bare arms looked skeletal in her sleeveless, pink, cotton top.

4

Neighborhood Watch

I gritted my teeth as my guts twisted. May's words tore through me like a knife, but I knew she was right. The voluntary ration system wasn't working. Individual greed had overcome the greater good. We were failing. The truth, I knew, was not greed but survival, a very human instinct in these circumstances. People in the neighborhood had been hoarding supplies for themselves, not sharing as we had all agreed.

At the neighborhood watch meeting convened a week after they arrived and cut off the power, representatives from every house in our subdivision agreed to work for the common good. Now that supplies were becoming scarce, it was becoming obvious not everyone was sharing everything.

If Oscar and his small force of four men and two women didn't return from the latest mission, it was bad news for the neighborhood. Several times, food- and medicine-scrounging missions had disappeared in the past two weeks. These volunteers were sent out heavily armed, with guns collected from the neighborhood residents for a collective armory. Their unexplained disappearance meant conditions outside the barricades we'd set up after the power grid failed were getting worse, or something too terrible to contemplate was happening. Our role as neighborhood leaders may have also broken down. I wished now Oscar hadn't agreed to lead this last mission himself, but he had explained that we as leaders needed to lead and show the people we accepted the same risks as everyone else.

Before he left, he told me privately he'd determine what had happened to the other teams if he could.

If our leadership failed to maintain control, then we'd fall into anarchy, survival of the fittest would surpass all other considerations, and we'd have a crisis on our hands. The thought of quelling an uprising of my friends and neighbors caused me many sleepless nights.

A few of the neighborhood men were former military, or reservists like Pete, who had skills with weapons. Many of these qualified former soldiers were manning the makeshift barricades, composed of trucks and cars that had been abandoned after the fuel supply was gone and various pieces of furniture, surrounding the perimeter of the ten block radius we were responsible for. So far, our internal communications system had been working.

We'd been using old analog, battery-operated walkie-talkies, but the supply of batteries, as with the food and water, was nearly exhausted.

Neighborhood Watch

Our neighborhood consisted of fifty homes originally containing two hundred and twenty-five residents. In the past six weeks, we'd lost thirty-five in total. Fifteen disappeared on supply missions, an equal number of the elderly and the very young were lost to starvation, suicides made up the balance of our losses. We were down to one hundred ninety warm bodies. Many were physically capable but I wasn't so sure about many of these peoples mental state.

Suddenly we heard footsteps pounding down the stairs from above us and Sue Burns burst into to the room, her breath coming in gasps, her lean arms and bare legs covered in a sheen of sweat. Her tan shorts and white top were sweat stained and greasy. Her green eyes were wild and unfocused by fear.

In her trembling right hand she held a walkie-talkie. In her left was the AR-15 semi-auto rifle I had given her after she completed firearms training two weeks ago.

"Sue," I said in a voice meant to calm her. "Calm down."

Sue nodded but her eyes flitted between the assembled leaders still seated at the table and she was avoiding making eye contact with me. Her breathing steadied but her worn Nikes still shifted side to side.

The woman was as jumpy as a cat on summer-heated blacktop.

I stood, then placed my hands on the sides of her narrow shoulders to steady her and stared into her eyes. "What's wrong, Sue?"

She finally looked at me, but her eyes were placid and eerily free of any emotion I could recognize. It was as if she was now at the center of a hurricane. "Uhhhh...there's a group of armed people approaching the north side of the barricades near Elmont Street," she said, her voice a dry hoarse whisper.

My breath caught in my throat. I looked over my shoulder at Pete, who had visibly tensed. "You and the others go ahead and check it out. I'll be along shortly."

Pete's tanned brow wrinkled and his eyes narrowed. He stood and signaled to the others to stand, too, then nodded. He hurried up the stairs with May and Alice close behind. I heard the echo of their footsteps *thump* up the stairs until there again was silence. Before they left the house, they would arm themselves and then head for the Elmont Street barricade.

I directed my attention to studying Sue's sweaty features.

Her shoulders sagged and I knew the adrenaline driving her was ebbing. I gently took the walkie-talkie from her and set it on the poker table. I then slipped my fingers around the barrel of the rifle gripped in her left hand, intending to take it from her as well.

Sue's normally placid, oval-shaped face shifted to anger, her eyes glaring at me. I sensed the strength returning to her lean frame. She pulled the gun away violently, forcing me to reluctantly release the weapon. In her present state, Sue was probably dangerous to herself and others.

This was confirmed when I saw the look in her eyes and knew she had lost touch with reality. For the first time since the beginning of the crisis, it occurred to me that a neighbor might shoot me. "Sue, tell me what's wrong." I spoke in an even tone so as not to spook her.

"I need the gun," she said between gritted teeth. I stepped back and gave her room, raising my hands in surrender.

"Why don't you sit and we'll talk?"

Sue's eyes narrowed and a bead of sweat ran down her sunburned cheek. "You're trying to trick me. You want my gun." She pointed the muzzle at me, her right index finger hovering over the trigger.

"I will kill you...anyone...who tries to take my gun." Her voice was low and threatening.

I smiled and sat down, placing my hands, one over the other, on the table and resting my weight on my forearms. "No, of course I won't take your gun. If you recall, I was the one who gave it to you." I kept my tone light.

Sue's features twisted in confusion, anger, and suspicion all at once. I'd succeeded in confusing her. Slowly she lowered the gun and dropped into the chair across from me, the AR-15 hanging loose at her side, the barrel pointed at the floor. She appeared exhausted, the last of her inner resources spent. A sense of relief washed over me.

I walked around the table until I stood beside her slumping body. Her eyelids were heavy with sleep. I carefully reached for the rifle and managed to gingerly release her now loose grip when she suddenly bolted upright, grabbing for the barrel. I pulled hard and wrested it away from her as she managed to stand, her face twisted by inner fury. Waves of intense hatred from Sue washed over me. I knew, if she managed to keep control of the gun, I was dead and then the others would be next. I had to take it from her. I had no choice.

Neighborhood Watch

It was as if the world was moving in slow motion. I took two steps backward as I raised the gun until it was level with her midsection. Without thinking, I pulled the trigger twice. Two loud bangs echoed off the walls and Sue's eyes went wide as she stumbled backward, gasping for breath. My nostrils and mouth were suddenly invaded by the smell of burnt gunpowder mingled with the iron scent of blood.

Sue clutched her stomach with both hands. Dark red blood seeped between her fingers. I froze. She looked at me, her eyes wide, the pain behind them making me want to wretch. I couldn't believe I'd shot my friend. *God, what have I done?*

I lowered the weapon, letting it fall from my grip. It rattled as it struck the floor. "Sue, I'm so sorry."

Sue's mouth hung open as blood started to trickle from the right side of her mouth. She dropped to her knees, then collapsed onto her bottom with a cry of pain. She moaned softly. I knelt beside her and wrapped one arm around her shoulders as she dropped backward. I sat on the floor, cradling her head in my lap. She looked up at me, her watery eyes filled with pain. Her mouth moved but I couldn't make out most of the words except for "Sorry."

Her eyes closed and her head lolled to one side as the air escaped from her lungs for the last time. I hugged her to me and began to cry, salty tears rolling down my cheeks.

"I'm sorry, so sorry, Susie, I didn't...." I was about to say I didn't mean to kill her, but that wasn't true. I'd had to stop her even if it meant killing her. It was like shooting a rabid dog. Sue had gone off the mental cliff and she wouldn't have come back. She could have killed us all.

I eased her off my lap and let her limp body roll on its side in the pool of blood that had formed around her before her heart stopped. I wiped the tears away from my eyes and stood.

A rush of anger formed a knot in my belly. Those bastards were at fault. *They* forced us to turn on each other. A lot of good people, a lot of Sue's, would still be alive if they hadn't come to our planet. *Goddamned aliens*.

***

The cement floor of the warehouse made the interior of the vast empty building cooler than the humid air outside.

Neighborhood Watch

I had my eyes closed as I fanned myself with one hand, grateful for the relief from the oppressive summer heat bearing down on the harbor beyond the open bay doors lining both sides of the structure. The warehouse sat at the end of a long pier, jutting out into the bay.

A cry of gulls filled my ears. I opened my eyes to gaze out the open bay door nearest me and spotted the gray wings of the snow-white birds circling above the overturned and burned-out ships floating untended in the oily water in the bay. Like the water, the air was still; but I could smell the rotting flesh of dead fish and human corpses entombed in those shattered vessels. The stench used to make me gag but I was well past that now—I was getting used to the odors of death. I'd seen too much of it in the past six weeks, more than most soldiers saw in a year on the battlefield. But we were on the frontline of the fight for survival, and one consequence was witnessing things no one should have to.

"Liz," called a man's voice from behind my left shoulder. I shifted on the steel chair to face him— Al Hamburg, in his battle armor, hefting his assault rifle. His curly blond hair stuck out from the edges of a Kevlar helmet and dark sunglasses covered his eyes.

His torso, arms, and legs were protected by body armor. He nodded at me when I didn't reply and disappeared from view behind the warehouse wall where he would stand guard until he escorted me back to the neighborhood. We were five miles from the barricades but I knew Al and his team would protect me. They had accompanied me from the barricade, where they'd shown up to escort me to this meeting. Professional soldiers always follow orders, so I wasn't worried.

Al was the commander of an elite Special Forces unit recruited by the Hsu-Zat to act as bodyguards when they visited our planet's surface. The Hsu-Zat had arrived in Earth orbit six weeks ago and immediately used some form of advanced electromagnetic pulse weapon to take out our technology worldwide. The weapon even used our satellites to send the pulse that threw civilization back into the dark ages. I missed my damned cell phone more than I should. I must have been addicted to the thing.

Airliners dropped from the sky, creating massive destruction and loss of life. Military forces so dependent on technology found themselves and their weapons useless.

Neighborhood Watch

Even the most EMP-hardened technology was ineffective in preventing this alien weapon from taking it out. The world had gone all to hell, and all that stood between anarchy and order was the neighborhood watch.

I know all this because, for some reason, a Hsu-Zat who called himself Robert—he told me his real name would be unpronounceable—decided I would be the spokesperson for my neighborhood. We'd met regularly, once per week, for the past six weeks. I'd never asked why he chose me, and frankly I didn't care.

The odd thing was Robert answered any question I asked him and had since our first meeting. As far as I could tell, everything he told me was accurate. The human tendency to lie to protect personal feelings didn't seem to apply to these aliens. He casually related the death toll numbers caused by their suppression of our technology and by the disruptions in civil order that soon followed.

If he considered my circumstances dire in any way, he hadn't let on. In fact, Robert had been cold but not unkind to me. That's why I'd left my knife behind, the one I had intended to use to slit his throat as retribution for Sue's death.

Even if I managed to kill him, one alien's death wouldn't mean much in the scheme of things.

From one of the open bay doors, Robert entered, flanked by two others of his kind. His crimson-colored features were placid, his two mustard-yellow eyes avoiding me as his brown boots slapped the concrete floor. The sound of the three aliens' footsteps echoed off the high walls. Other than their skin color, they were humanoid: two arms, two legs, everything in the same places as us. It had been difficult for me to distinguish one alien from another until I noticed the small scar on the end of Robert's pointed chin. He later told me this was due to a childhood fall without elaborating further.

His dark blue slacks and brown vest covered a frame that looked lean and strong, yet his voice had always been gentle, reminding me of the sound of a stream rushing over a rocky bottom. His arms were bare, as was his hairless head. His ears were relatively human shaped, the curvature at the top slightly elongated. His companions were dressed in identical garb. *There must have been a big sale on alien fashions at the Hsu-Zat Walmart.*

Robert stopped in front of me. His long arms, hanging loosely at his sides, ended with elongated fingers near his knees.

Neither he nor his escorts had even been seen carrying weapons. *Ray guns obviously aren't his team's thing.*

One of his escorts went to grab another steel chair from ten feet across the warehouse floor. He carried it back, placing it behind Robert, who immediately sat, his eyes finally landing on mine.

"Hello, Elizabeth," he said in his usual monotone.

"Robert," I said with a slight nod of my head.

His eyes crinkled slightly at the corners. "I am saddened to learn of Susan's death."

I don't know how he knew, but Al probably told him before the meeting. I had learned not to trust those Special Forces guys. As far as I was concerned, they were the aliens' pets.

His words seemed genuine. Robert had either won the Hsu-Zat equivalent of the best actor Oscar or he meant what he'd said. I prefer to think it was the latter because he had never before shown any remorse for the deaths they had caused. At our next meeting, I decided, I would reverse my earlier decision. This son of a bitch was dead. I would probably die too, but the satisfaction would be better than a gold card with an unlimited credit limit.

"I am leaving," Robert said next.

"But you just got here," I said sarcastically.

Robert hesitated and his eyes shifted to an open bay door to his right and the ocean beyond. I glanced out the door. The wind had picked up and small swells had formed in the harbor. The cooling breeze brushed my right cheek. I detected the now familiar smells of almonds and orange coming from the aliens as the wind swirled through the warm air of the warehouse.

Robert's yellow eyes finally drifted back to mine. "Please forgive me. I meant we are leaving for home earlier than expected."

May's words echoed in my mind and my heart skipped a beat. "You said we had ninety days then you'd turn the power back on."

Robert nodded. "Yes, I did, but my orders have changed. I must return home immediately." The alien stared at me, his eyes pleading. He was unable to elaborate. I glanced at his companions and saw them standing stiff as soldiers at attention, their eyes focused straight ahead looking into the distance, appearing uninterested in our conversation. But I knew they were very interested and listening to every word.

"Will you at least turn the power back on?"

Robert shook his head. "No, that is beyond our capability."

I pursed my lips as my gut tightened. The bastards told us when they destroyed the grids they would restore them after ninety days. It hadn't made sense at the time, but what choice did we have but to believe them. Obviously they lied. "When are you leaving?"

"Immediately," he said again. He paused and I could tell his next words were very uncomfortable for him. I braced myself for the worst. "There are nuclear power generating facilities all across your world that are going critical without the power grid. These facilities will soon melt down and send clouds of radioactive material into your atmosphere. Unfortunately, this means all life on your planet will be extinguished."

My stomach churned and my emotions threatened to overwhelm me. Fear, anger, love, hate ebbed and flowed through my mind. "Then what was the ninety days all about?"

For the first time since I'd met him, Robert appeared flustered. His features were a darker red, his skin now the color of pomegranate juice. His hands trembled and his eyes sagged, reflecting a very human sadness. "I'm sorry," he said again. "Orders."

I nodded and sighed. He wasn't a bad guy for an alien. "Okay, Robert." I stood and his two companions suddenly stepped between us. I smirked at the three aliens, then turned and walked away.

The ninety days was in realty a countdown. A countdown to doomsday. The Hsu-Zat had known all along what would happen after they shut down everything. Their arrival was an experiment and we were the guinea pigs.

Once the human race was extinct, the aliens would eventually have a green and fertile planet to colonize without interference from the indigenous population. Sure, it would take time for the Earth's ecosystems to regenerate, but the Hsu Zat had all time in the universe. Our time had run out. Maybe Sue was one of the lucky ones.

I was determined to delay our impending doom, at least in my little corner of the world. The neighborhood watch would continue maintaining some semblance of civilization until the end came. We weren't going quietly into the night.

While it was more likely we'd destroy ourselves before the radioactive clouds killed us, the neighborhood watch would forestall the inevitable as long as possible. Our neighborhood would stand alone if need be.

As for me, I was determined to be the leader I was born to be. I wasn't about to give the Hsu Zat our neighborhood without showing them we still had fight left in us. It's what we humans do

Until We Meet Again

Human history becomes more and more a race between education and catastrophe. - H. G. Wells

April 17, 2031

ITS THOUGHTS FLOWED THROUGH HIS MIND.

It knows everything.

An alarm warbled through the empty corridors of the underground installation deep below the Oregon desert. All sensation disappeared as the room was lost to a black void, a starless night. Silence. The remnants of the alarms echo washed over him. Secure. Nothing in, nothing out.

In the stifling darkness Ira Newfeld slid down the wall, his sweat soaked back slick against the cool porcelain tile. He sat statue like on the lab floor. The only sound now was his own breathing as he felt another malodorous trickle of sweat run down his lean face. The others are finished.

A heavy pounding began that came from the secured inner door of the testing room. The door, composed of two inches of hardened steel with re-enforced hinges, meant it wouldn't be able to get to him.

General Walters ordered the evacuation. Too late. Now they were all gone, he was alone and Ira knew he needed to let someone in the outside world know before it was too late for him.

He froze to listen to the sound of tortured steel being rendered followed by the crash of the door slapping hard against the tiled lab floor. Then all sound again ceased. Ira's heart beat furiously in his ears.

"Ira," a whispered voice called his name.

Ira held his breath a scream caught in his throat. He knew then he wouldn't be warning anyone about what was happening here.

"Come out, come out, wherever you are," whispered the voice in his mind. He listened to the muffled echo of footsteps that moved slowly toward him.

***

If you want to make an apple pie from scratch, you must first create the universe. - Carl Sagan

January 25, 2033

"They're all dead," says President Romana Wilson, her voice flat.

I'm stunned. "Everyone?"

I'm in a window less conference room with the president and two men I don't recognize. The walls are decorated with paintings of various presidents dating back at least two hundred years. The table is twenty feet long and the room large enough for the cabinet to hold their meetings. But there are only us four present.

President Wilson nods to indicate I should take a seat then crosses her arms across her chest, her gray eyes flicker as I sit across from her. Her tan suit looks like it's been pressed and her yellow blouse is the color of spring daisies in bloom.

MY stomach knots. Since I'm the only scientist attending this meeting it means I'm all that remains of the original Phoenix Project team. I know why she wants me in particular. Whatever she's up to involves the infamous project, and its hell spawned offspring, and I know with absolute certainty I want no part of it.

"I want nothing to do with any project involving Phoenix. I thought I made that clear…"

"Oh, we won't be going back to that again."

25

The look in her eye says she's attempting to bait me and it works.

"I don't understand…" I say my eyes narrowing as I gaze at her shimmering image. She turns and speaks softly to someone off camera then turns again to face the camera.

"Rather than just telling you, how about I show you?" She smiles at me her eyes hard. I'm about to object and tell her there's no way I'm leaving the Lark when she must've guessed what I was about to say because she says, "Before you jump ship I'll have a presentation you must see then you can judge where we go from here. Okay?" She arches one eyebrow.

I indicate my agreement with nod. The president smiles grimly then she shifts her eyes to one of the silent men and indicates with a wave of one hand to proceed. The lights in the room dim then the holo-presentation begins. What I see makes my jaw drop. It's the end of the world, at least for the human race.

When the presentation ends, the room is suddenly cold even though I know the temperature controls haven't been altered. The image shimmers again and Romana stands before me only this time she's leaning against her desk with her arms crossed across her chest, her expression grim.

"Bill, I know how you feel about this, but we have a real problem on our hands and we need your help. I mean it, Bill. Without the intervention outlined in the presentation the human race will die out within fifty years."

I gaze at her dumfounded by this news. I'll be dead by then but so will everyone man, woman, and child on the planet. "Romana, I will help if I can. I don't know though if we have time."

She nods and the tension in her shoulders visibly relaxes. "The project is called Brahma, after the Hindu God of creation, headquartered in a small town in Oregon."

I gaze at her overwhelmed by a sense of puzzlement. The sides of her mouth curled up and her mouth forms a slight smile.

"Don't worry we've set up a fully equipped laboratory and staffed it with the best of our remaining geneticists…" she pauses to take a breath and the slight smile fades and her eyes become hard. Obviously something she hasn't said continues to upset her. "You and Dr. Khanna will be sequestered there until you have perfected the technology to stem this threat. The two agents I dispatched will take you to the lab so you can begin work."

The holo-projector goes dark startling me with the abrupt termination of the image. I'm wondering who or what is this Dr. Khanna?

"Olsen and I'll wait here, sir while you get ready," says World Security Institute Agent Paul Watson with a smug expression on his young face. He's obviously pleased that the first part of their mission is successful. The clone cops are an impatient lot. The two agents delivered the message-holo from Romana.

I change into my softest blue jeans, worn red and blue work shirt and my favourite walking shoes, the brown leather ones, very comfortable for long trips, and pad again into the hallway.

I'm met by the two agents in the lobby. They stand the moment they see me and I detect they're anxious. I note the way Watson glances at his watch when he sees me and I realize that his calm, take your time demeanour is a cover for his urgency.

I shrug, why should I give a shit about their timetable? "Okay, guys let's haul ass." I hook my thumbs off the pockets of my black jeans.

***

January 26, 2033
Wisdom begins in wonder. -Socrates

The salty wind hits me full in the face when I step out of the limousine onto the potholed gravel parking lot. The drive from Portland International took two hours too long for me. I already hated the place even before I got here, wherever in hell here is. A ragged looking seagull screams as it floats into the strong wind overhead, that comes toward me full force off the wild ocean. The vast horizon is consumed by white-topped surf. A long stretch of gray beach runs north and south as far as I can see. What little grass grows on the embankment is sparse and the color of dry straw.

The shack that stands in the middle of the parking lot is dilapidated and seems ready to collapse under its own weigh with one more gust of raw wind.

I pull the dark knee length raincoat Agent Watson gave me on the plane tighter about me. "How am I supposed to work in there?" I shout to be heard above the howl of the wind.

"That's an elevator building, doc. The lab is below ground." Watson waves me toward the structure. I shrug and follow him, after all I've come this far why not at least see the place?

Once inside the building, the outward appearance being a clever deception, the wind stops.

The reception area, staffed by an armed guard who sits granite like behind a wall of surveillance monitors stands as we enter. He requests our identification. Watson gives me a temporary security pass with a digital picture he'd made during the flight affixed to it. I feel the guard's eyes on me as he studies the picture then my face, at least I now know what a microbe feels like. He slips the card through a scanning device, the strip on the back is encoded with my DNA, and there are two indicator lights, one red and one green. The red light comes on after he's run my card.

He looks up, with a look of someone very serious about their chosen profession, and hands me back my card. "Thank you, sir."

The guard repeats the procedure with Watson and Olsen, two more red lights and we're cleared to proceed to the lower levels. A color coded chart next to the elevators doors tells me that the underground portion of the facility below ground contains over thirty levels.

"Where are we going?" I ask. Watson turns his head slightly to glance at me and a small smile crosses his lips.

"To the bottom." He points to the purple floor on the chart with one index finger then turns away and presses the down button.

I feel a vague sense of unease as I stand between the two agents. I'm about to go way over my head, literally.

***

We're going to turn this team around 360 degrees. - Jason Kidd

My mind so whirls with possibilities that I fail to notice our stop at the lowest level. The doors slide open and we step into another lobby, the walls glow white, back lit by rows of florescent bulbs. Another uniformed guard stands behind a reception desk recessed into the floor identical to the one at ground level. His swarthy, grim features study us as we approach and I note his eyes travel over our security passes then our faces his eyes examining ours for any sign of trouble. These guys are careful.

"Watson, WSI." He motions toward me. "This is Dr. Lumberman."

Then guard nods silently then plucks a hand held communicator from the desktop and speaks softly into the device. Even though I am close to him I fail to make out the words.

It isn't long before a brown skinned man wearing a wide smile appears from a hidden door in the wall behind the stoic guard. He is dressed in a black turtleneck, blue jeans, brown leather loafers, his lean form covered by a knee length white lab coat.

Above the lab coats breast pocket is a plastic name tag that tells me he is the mystery man of the hour, Dr. Khanna. I smile and take his firm grip in mine.

"Dr. Khanna, where's your badge, sir?" says the guard giving the new arrival a disapproving glare.

Khanna shrugs and reaches into a pocket of his lab coat and pulls his identification badge. The guard nods obviously satisfied. Khanna grimaces at me. "We all need to wear them. Sorry, it's nothing really just can't be too careful."

Khanna leads me through the door. Watson doesn't follow us so I assume his job was over for now. Much to his relief I'm sure.

Once inside I'm shocked to see the number of work stations each with its an electron microscope, protein synthesizer, protein sequencer, DNA synthesizer and DNA sequencer. The sophistication of this laboratory is truly impressive I don't recall ever seeing such compact technology in a genetics lab before.

At the end of the room, which I estimate is the size of a football field, and equally as wide, is a wall made of smoked glass that separates the lab from another room. The room on the other side of the glass must be dark, because no light escapes from the inside.

The lighting in the lab itself comes from rows of florescent tube boxes hung from the ceiling. The light box covers diffuse the light to give the room a gentle haze like quality.

I move to the first station and gaze at the sophistication of the gene sequencer. The compatibility of the new models is inspired genius compared with the much larger one I worked with during the Phoenix project. One thing bothers me though.

"Dr. Khanna, this is all very impressive, but why so much equipment?"

Khanna smiles warmly and crosses his arms. "That didn't take long." He sighs heavily. "Dr. Lumberman…"

"Bill, please…"

"Of course…Bill." He continues, "We modify gene sequences to build a better human by adding foreign DNA—"

"That's bull shit." I interrupt him. "We tried that during Phoenix and it failed.

"Every time we tried to introduce a new gene other than human the sequence became non-viable, no matter what the type of DNA."

Khanna shrugs. "Yes I know, I read the research, but what if I told you we found a way safely introduce foreign DNA that works."

"I'd say you were a liar."

Dr. Khanna's dark eyebrows go up and he grins, with a twinkle behind his eyes. "Is seeing believing?" I nod.

"Well then, Bill, follow me." He turns and heads away toward the wall of smoked glass. I follow gripped by curiosity. What he's talking about is nonsense science. I wonder where Romana got this guy? I didn't seem to recall reading his name in any of the serious journals. Maybe he's one of those self-professed experts so often quoted in the supermarket tabloids.

I stare at the wall of dark glass unable to see anything on the other side when it begins to swirl as if churned into motion be some unseen whirlpool. Larger swirls form in the glass wall and the smoke begins to dissipate. Light begins to show through until there are patches of clear areas forming. Finally I see what is hidden on the other side. There is a woman seated at a clear glass table eating a bowl of soup.

I can see the steam rising from the red liquid (very likely tomato) as she spoons the hot soup into her wide mouth, between full lips. She wears a brilliant white jumpsuit that covers her lean body and her poker straight hair is the color of motor oil, sleek and long falling about half down her back. Her eyes are a brilliant green, unusual for someone with such dark features. She must be no more than twenty years old.

It's difficult to tell what her ethnic background is, she looks part Asian, Slavic and Italian all in equal proportion, strange yet exotic at the same time.

"This is Kya," says Khanna his eyes glow with obvious pride.

I watch her for a few minutes noting her vacant stare at the wall, no looking side to side, no interest in anything but a blank wall. She doesn't even seem to be interested in the soup. With one hand in her lap while the other spoons each spoonful of soup with mechanical precision then the spoon drops to the bowl ready to take its next excursion. Not one drop is spilled during this process.

"Is she alive?" I ask.

Khanna chuckles. "Of course she is, she's our test subject. Don't you recognize her?"

My eyes narrow as I study the young woman. I shake my head.

"Bill, she's the only viable embryo left from the Phoenix project. We needed a baseline for the new generation you and I will construct under the new program. She's worked out very well, yes, very well indeed."

My skin grows cold. "You mean you took one of my genomes? We destroyed them."

Khanna shakes his head.

I watch the young woman for a few moments unable to speak, the words caught in my throat, finally I say, "Let's say your telling me the truth, which I highly doubt until I see the data, and let's say this woman is a fully realized clone from a marriage of human and foreign DNA, what is the difference between her and the last generation of clones."

"Bill, didn't you read the reports I sent with Watson?"

"No, I don't read reports I like to see the facts for myself."

Khanna faces me and frowns. "Hmmm…that's unfortunate." He pauses. "It's like this; we were able to adapt extraterrestrial DNA to enhance this woman. She's a hybrid and much a more advanced human being than has ever lived."

***

Every great advance in science has issued from a new audacity of imagination. -John Dewey

To say I'm in shock is the understatement of all time. Romana's presentation said human DNA is breaking down due to the high pollution levels in Earth's ecosystem.

We're on the brink of poisoning our environment and ourselves out of existence. The technology to move our people to another planet doesn't exist so we were about to disappear from the universe forever. The presentation ended by saying that Project Brahma, without any specifics, will create a new breed of human that will adapt quicker to the future biosphere and extend our lives until the environmental problem was overcome by new technologies, but alien DNA? *Were these people nuts?*

"Where did you get the alien DNA?" I say. We're seated at one end of a long steel table in the automated cafeteria being served our dinner by one of the servo-bots. The room is large enough that our voices echo off the walls. I'm eating broiled gen-chicken with a side salad and Dr. Khanna (who urged me to call him Marty, an anglicized version of his real name Momar) a vegetable curry. The pungent curry smell permeates the room preventing my enjoyment of the chicken.

It's a shame really they certainly don't serve anything this expensive at the Lark.

"Actually I don't know." He looks embarrassed by his lack of knowledge.

"You mean to say you introduce a foreign life form into our DNA not knowing where it originated and the possible ramifications?"

He nods and his eyes drop to his plate of greenish curry.

I feel the anger begin in the pit of my stomach. These people are playing with fire and they don't even seem to care. I decided to withhold judgement until I've reviewed the data. "Let's see the records after dinner."

He nods again unable, or unwilling, to make eye contact.

After the servo-bots have removed our dishes we head for the lab to review the data. The wall of glass is fogged again, though having seen the wall become translucent I am able to discern the swirls of dancing rainbow of color that now obscures our view of Kya. As I sit behind one of the workstations, and the computer monitor lifts from a hidden compartment that appears in the smooth black surface of the station, I hear a strange voice echo in my mind. It's as if a fleeting breeze has crossed my thoughts brushing against me. I shiver from the mental touch. Maybe the lab is haunted.

Dr Khanna sits on a three-wheeled stool off my left shoulder watching me. His long arms are crossed.

"So, Marty, why all these stations for just the two of us?" This had been bothering me since I arrived.

"There were twenty-seven members of the project team working here when I joined the project." Getting this guy to give up information is like breaking your leg just before a once in a lifetime vacation, you just want to scream.

"Yes, but where are they now?" I hold up my hands to show I wasn't getting it.

"Dead," he says in an unemotional tone.

I whirl in my seat to face him. His brown eyes are watery. "What? How?"

"She did it." Now normally I would assume he meant Kya expect she looked about as benign as the clone cat at the Lark.

"Surely not, Kya."

His brown eyes abruptly came up to fix on mine. I knew immediately. Somehow that exotic young woman killed the entire project team, but...

"How did they die?"

"Two years ago. Their minds were *eaten*."

"Eaten?"

He nods. "That's about the only way I can describe what happened to them. When the security force managed to get into the lab they found the corpses untouched, no blood, no signs of violence, Kya was the only survivor, other than Ira Newfeld."

Newfeld? That surprised me, but why only him?

Marty continues to explain, "During the autopsy I ran some detailed memory scans on the bodies, you know with the new ones that show the last forty eight hours before the memory engrams lose integrity then they fade. I discovered the memory receptors were empty. Everything wiped, gone. I coined the term, eaten."

"Where's Newfeld?"

Marty shakes his head his eyes drop away. "He died two days after he was retrieved. Probably for the best really, he was in pretty bad shape. What was left of his mind was barely enough to keep his organs functioning. He didn't have the wherewithal to hit the self destruct switch."

I gaze at Marty and he glances at me and shrugs. "I'll show you where the switch is later, just in case."

I don't appreciate his lackadaisical attitude but what am I going to do? I'm here and I have to do something to save the human race.

My concern right now revolves around Kya and her mysterious abilities.

I decide to change tact, "Is Kya a telepath?"

Marty stares at me, his face twisted by conflicting emotions. "How do you know this?"

"I felt her."

Marty smirks. "Now who's the liar?"

"I felt something or someone brush my mind."

"Impossible."

"Why?" Now we are getting somewhere.

"I installed a chip to control her telepathic ability. She cannot…" he pauses and his eyes narrow. "I will make sure," he says curtly.

Marty shows me the emergency panel where the autodestruct switch is located. It's a rather mundane looking black button on the panel that might be connected to the lights for all I can tell, not that I know what to expect it to look like. Maybe I expect the word 'DANGER' in big red letters, or something, the only label underneath the switch says ERT (and in tiny letters beneath it, so small I need my reading glasses to see them, it reads Emergency Response Tracker). Marty tells me that once activated the entire laboratory complex will be open to the sea within seconds and everyone inside will be drowned.

The walls contain thousands of baseball size ducts, which lead to the Pacific Ocean, barely twenty feet from where we stand. I feel a sense of unease at this bit of information and immediately gain respect for the nondescript switch.

After this I return to my quarters to rest. I lay on my single bunk staring at the ceiling trying to absorb what I've learned today.

If Kya is a hybrid of human and alien then what do we need her for? And more importantly what do they need me for? They seem to have her under control. I feel a sudden jolt run through my body as a powerful mind touches mine.

They need you to make more of me and solve the telepathy problem.

I feel as if I'm losing my mind but I respond to the voice. "How is telepathy a problem? I don't understand."

You will. Silence. I expect the walls to cave in any second but nothing happens.

I make my way to the lab and fail to find Marty. Where could he be? I walk up to the wall of smoked glass and the swirling mass of color begins to dissipate. I see Marty lying face down on the floor inside the enclosure. I start as I see Kya, her dark eyes study me as if I were the fish in a fishbowl.

He's dead, says the voice which I knew to be Kya's.

"Why?"

Like Dr. Newfeld he thought I was his private guinea pig. I am not.

"That much is obvious, Kya, but did he deserve to die?" She shrugs her narrow shoulders and a small smile crosses her full lips. I feel as if I'm in a trance, mesmerized by those two tepid pools of green. I know what I must do. I have no choice. If I fail the horror of what Khanna…no, what I, created will be set loose upon the world. It seems that the end of the human race is inevitable, a testament to our arrogance. I struggle against her mind as I make my way along the wall to the emergency panel. My finger hesitates over the switch that will end my life's work. I feel the invader grip my mind and my body shakes with wave after wave of torment she rains down on me. With a rush of realization I know now why they need me. Romana and the damned clone cops know I'm the only Phoenix member left with a conscience. I'll make the correct choice.

They know I'm the only person on Earth willing to stop Kya before she's able to rip my mind away. They know I have abilities that no one else has, damn them.

I don't want to do this. My hand trembles while rivers of sweat obscure my vision as I reach for the switch.

Have to stop her. I will…

It knows.

It ends.

***

For of all sad words of tongue or pen, the saddest are these: It might have been! - John Greenleaf Whittier

Nineteenth day of 47th year of the Order of Jera

Excerpt report: Survey 13781, Leader Motal Telo:

Latal sector the third planet, Zon class star.

Damage to ecosystem as follows:

Scans confirm, planetary atmosphere unable to support life.

Life improbable given the current conditions.

Recommendations:

Abandon research project this sector until ecosystem self repairs.

Next survey: 160th year of the Order of Kir.

End report.

One Day At A Time

ELLEN STOOD WEARING HER PURPLE FLEECE NIGHT gown on her long, wide back deck facing the Inlet with a steaming cup of coffee in her hand looking out at the water.

It was such a mild morning on the Sunshine coast on this first week of January, she couldn't believe how fortunate they were this year. It seemed that they had escaped any snow at all.

Only a few cold days of below freezing at night, just enough to set her spring flowering blubs was all they'd had. She looked over at the side yard at the buds on her magnolia that were swelling and the roses that she had planted last summer, they were still in bloom only four weeks ago.

Then her eyes glanced at the lads, their dogs, playing tag in the back yard. One Samson, a seven-year-old golden retriever and the other a small fourteen year-old red terrier, Rusty.

The heavy rains they had for the last two week had stopped so today would be a good day to stretch their legs, they all needed a walk.

She looked back out at the water, she never tired of looking at the keyhole view they had of the Georgia Straight, the stretch of water between themselves and Vancouver Island. A well-seasoned sailboat captain had told her that there were only about eight miles of water between Gibsons and the large Vancouver Island. All she knew was when she and Lee, her husband of twenty-five years had seen this little two story home with it's level entry and walk out basement they knew they had found home.

There was lots of room for family and guests and the tall evergreen and arbutus trees that surrounded it made if feel cozy, their little cabin in the woods.

As she watched the water, she realized that something was wrong. In all the time they had lived here you could get to the water by walking a long set of wooden stairs.

Kelly leaned over the railing and looked at the waves between the trees on the right side of her view. The waves were coming from the west usually that meant fair weather, but something stank, really, badly.

It wasn't the pulp mill, they got the odd smell from there a couple of times a year.

No, this was like Oyster Bay at very low tide, mud, dead shellfish, oysters, muscles and seaweed. It made you want to heave.

She had never, ever no matter how low the tide got had seen the bottom. There was always water covering the rocks and gravel directly below them, but not this morning.

She'd left the television on when she checked the weather station and now she heard the emergency signal. At least that's what she thought it was. She called to the dogs as she went back into the house and looked at the large television in the corner of the living room between the bay window and the built in mantel over the wood-burning fireplace.

She heard Matthew her three-year-old grandson getting up and coming into the living room and gave him a quick smile. "Honey, why don't you go and find Grandpa? Tell him I want to see him right now. Hurry please," she said. She tried to emphasize the words without scaring Matthew. The boy scooted away as the announcer came on.

"A comet hit the Pacific ocean this morning.

"We are expecting earth quakes in the next few minutes and tidal waves to batter the Pacific Northwest this late morning, especially the area from San Francisco to Canada," said a man who could barley contain his fear.

Ellen quickly turned off the television in case Mathew heard what was happening. She looked to the telephone should she try and call Mathew's parents? She had to at least try. Then she'd make a quick call to her other son too. She picked up the cordless phone and started to dial. All she got was a busy signal even before she finished the phone number. She put it down on the kitchen counter.

Oh God, please not that.

She had heard so much about tsunamis from her friends in Oregon, all she could do is repeat what they had said to her over and over again. Get to higher ground. Get to higher ground. It was litany that kept repeating in her head. Kelly felt herself start to panic and then her rational brain kicked in. You can panic later, but right now you need to act.

"Lee, I need you to come up right now! I mean right now!" she called down to the basement. She hoped he heard her, he had to come now.

They had at most five minutes to leave and get to higher ground. She checked her watch.

Okay go.

Once the earthquakes started there was no telling how the road around her would hold up and they had to get out before the tidal wave.

What do you need? And I mean need? She thought the herself as she went through her list of must have things.

She ran into the guest bedroom and grabbed a large wheeled backpack. She was like a mad woman as she ran through the house opening drawers. Grabbing three of for each of them, three socks and underwear, three tee shirts, three pants, running shoes and hiking boots. She grabbed the dog bowls, their kibble, luckily they had just gotten more the other day and their treats.

They had to get out of here. Don't dawdle she thought as she ran into the living room and grabbed the photos and albums off the mantel and the antique oak mirrored hutch.

The best place would be the Safeway parking lot at the junction of Pratt and Gibsons Road. It was very high ground and she knew that this whole area was on a massive granite vein of rock that stretched for about fifty to one hundred miles all down the coast.

The dogs came bounding into the house, barking, happy to be able to play without the benefit of the dark days and heavy rains that they had been having, which was typical of a winter in Gibsons.

She ran and slammed closed the sliding glass patio door so the dogs couldn't get out.

"Lee, I need you here right now!" Kelly yelled all pretense of niceness gone. She tried to weight her odds of how many people would be trying to get to Safeway to find safety and food and water.

She heard the basement door open and Mathew's light little boy's voice chatting to his grandfather as they came up the stairs.

"What's the problem Ellen? We're coming," he said as he walked up the stairs with her budging laptop bag in his hand. He looked over the banister and saw her dragging the case with their clothes to the front door.

He took one look at her and quickly walked to her side and put an arm around her. "What is it, one of the kids?" he asked softly in her ear.

"No, worse, much worse. A comet has hit the Pacific Ocean, there's going to be tidal waves and earthquakes.

"There talking like the San Andrade's Fault
it finally going to let loose too," said Ellen as she
watched Lee's eyes got softer as she spoke so fast
most people would not be able to understand her.
Then he looked around the foyer and by the front
door, licked his lips and nodded.

"I know. I've got my lap-top and the mini
tower," he said a as he walked into their pantry, pulled
out a large cloth shopping bag went down the hall and
pulled down three of his favorite paintings that she
had done over the years.

"We need to get to higher ground right now,"
they said in unison.

"They said they don't know when things are
going to happen but I figure we've got five minutes.
Listen carefully," she said looking at her wristwatch.
"We've used three of the already.

She quickly went through the things she had
packed from flashlights with extra batteries to toilet
paper and everything in between. He listened as
she spoke and they started to carry things to the tan
colored RAV4 they would be taking with them.

"Can you think of anything else? I don't
have fresh water so I used some of our buckets and a
couple of pots with tap water. I'm hoping to get some
more water at the grocery store."

Ellen had to stop for a minute, she was breathing so hard and her mouth was so dry she was starting to get dizzy.

Lee put his arms around her and held her in his arms. "It's going to be okay. We have Vancouver Island to take the brunt off the tidal action and as for earth quakes as you told me when we bought the house the huge granite vein under us and Mt. Capstone behind us has stood for many years and will be here for a very long time to come. We'll see how the house and your Studio do," he laughed softly as he gently pushed her short dark brown hair from her face and kissed her forehead.

They looked at each other nodded and quickly pulled the rest of the things out of the front door and into the back of the Rave.

In Ellen's head she kept on hearing, *get to higher ground, get to higher ground.* "We are, we are," she mumbled under her breath to herself.

Lee and Ellen picked up Mathew, strapped him into his car seat in the back seat and then Ellen armed with a pocket full of dog treats grabbed Rusty and threw him in the rear foot well with a treat then grabbed Samson and put him the back seat too.

As she was going to close the back door, Mathew started to cry and kick his feet.

"It's okay Mathew, we're going on a car ride up to Safeway, " she said as she leaned forward and pick up a toy that had fallen onto the seat, as she did Samson decided that he would squeeze past her and he started to head up the driveway.

Ellen's heart almost stopped. She knew that Samson had been really bad lately about coming when called. She could feel her stomach clench and her mind jumped to 'what might happen'.

She had to get him in the car now. They had to leave NOW! T

hey had to get to hire ground. Above all else they had to keep Mathew safe. And that might mean leaving Samson behind. She felt her eyes swell with tears and her vision blurred. She prepared herself, she'd have to live with whatever happened.

She only had one chance before they left.

"Okay, Sampson. Come," she said with authority.

Sampson walked to the top of the driveway and sniffed their hedge. She shook the dog treats. "Sampson. Cookie."

The dog looked up at her and slowly wagged his tail, his tongue lolled out from the side of his mouth. Great the dog was grinning at her thinking it was a game.

She felt Rusty jump up onto the back seat of the RAV. "Sampson, car ride. Cookie."

In her heart Ellen was begging for Sampson to come. She turned her back to the dog, shook the bad of treats and gave Rusty another cookie making sure that Sampson could see what she was doing. "Please God, please," she whispered under her breath, begging for the big dog to come.

"Get in the truck Ellen. He's wondering down the street," said Lee in a resigned, but firm voice.

She knew that she could just walk up to him and get him, but he was wandering to far away now. He'd gone a block and a half and they only had a few precious moments. She couldn't risk all their lives.

She closed the rear door and quickly walked around the truck and slid into the front passenger seat. She held back the tears, she would never forgive herself for leaving Samson, her big goofy buddy. She could feel sobs fill her chest and tears fill her eyes, she looked out of the window and tried to swallow her grief.

Maybe they would find him after this was all over. He knew the area because of their walks together, and he was smart. She bet that he'd get home before they would, but her tears wouldn't stop.

"Okay let's go!" she said as she put on her seatbelt and slammed the door closed. She took a deep breath and held onto the armrest.

Lee stepped on the gas, nothing happened. Lee tried again, but the car wouldn't start. Nothing. This had never happened to her before. He looked at Ellen. She glanced at him as she opened her door and jumped out.

"It won't start. Look grab Mathew and start up Third Street I'll meet you at Safeway or along the road," said Lee as he looked at Ellen.

She almost laughed at the suggestion. Yea, she could get a short way up the hill, but not all the way to the highway, but it was a good four to five miles away. Would she get there with a small three-year-old boy in tow in the next few minutes. Not a chance.

"Come on get out. I'll get the car going," she said. She stood to the side and Lee jumped out. She slid behind the wheel, waved her remote control key, stepped on the brake firmly, and then hit the start button once it went green.

A welcoming deep rumble greeted their ears as the car sprang to life.

"Okay, let's try this again," said Ellen and she got into her seat.

She looked up and noticed that the steady traffic in front of their door had slowed and then stopped.

"Lee, let's go up Third and then swing up Robin. I have a feeling that the traffic is plugged on Ocean View. Besides we'll constantly be going up and getting higher," said Ellen as she cleared her throat.

Lee checked the radio, there was only static on all the stations twice and nothing was on any of them, he turned it off.

"Gram, breakfast?" asked Mathew who had been very quiet up to now.

"Sure how about a nice soft blueberry bar and some water?" Ellen asked as she pulled up the large bag of snacks, juice and their small amount of bottled water. She opened a bar and handed it to him.

Ellen, rolled down her window, everything was eerily quiet. No bird song, no chitterling from squirrels, no eagles cry. She looked up, no birds, the only thing moving were the trees swaying with the wind.

"We'll go as far as we can. The Safeway lot is probably full right now. Any ideas?" asked Lee as he kept the truck steadily moving.

Suddenly the truck started to sway.

A huge sixty foot maple tree in front of them started to lean and then fall. The crash shook the truck luckily it fell away from the road. Lee stopped and waited. There were only a few cars before and behind them, they all stopped as well. They continued crawling forward and arrived at the corner of Overlook and Proud and turned left. They had passed by the steep switchbacks and the s-curves on Overlook now the road was straight all the way up to the main highway, where the Safeway was.

They drove up Proud slowly there were cars and trucks in the ditch, people walking up the road carrying children and belongings. They would occasionally look behind them at the water then back toward the mountain where they were heading.

They were about a mile away from the Safeway when another earthquake hit, this time the telephone poles across the street started to fall like dominoes along the road and not across it, they kept on moving. So far so good.

"I don't think that we'll have much of a problem here in Gibsons. At least not at first. The house may even be standing. It probably won't have any glass windows left, and we won't have electricity, but I'm hoping that we still have the a working septic tank.

"But I guess we need electricity for that, don't we?"

Lee nodded as he watched the road and the other cars around him waiting for another quake to hit them.

"I am worried about the kids, and our family and friends in Vancouver. I think some places will be fine. Don't you?"

"I know, I'm worried too. Look out the window, can you see the ocean from here? Maybe it won't be as bad as they predict. I'm worried about the ferries," said Lee letting Ellen's question hang.

Ellen craned her head toward the water. "I don't see any… oh, now I see water. It's about half way across to the Island. I can't see what's happening on the other side of the Island in the Long Beach area. I sure hope they get clear of all this. Mathew's asleep."

Lee nodded as they were buffeted again, this time harder and the truck slid to the right. He stopped, waited, and then proceeded slowly.

"Sason. Sason, where is he?" asked a sleepy Mathew as he woke and stretched. He started to sniffle as he looked around. "I want Sason. Here Sason!"

Ellen looked at Lee and saw tears in his eyes that he brushed away with the back of his hand. She swallowed hard trying to keep herself from getting emotional. "What do I say? How do I tell him that we just left Samson?"

"No. It's like we said, Samson went for a walk, he's exploring and we hope he's at home by the time we get back."

Ellen nodded and used her fingers to the rub the tears from her eyes. She felt like such a failure. She should have done something, she should have trained the dog better. But if that dog, no, when that dog came back he would be so trained no one would recognize him. She'd make sure of it.

"Honey, Samson went exploring, remember? Hopefully he'll be finished and at home when we get there. Do you want some water now? She reached back and unscrewed the bottle. Remember only a little bit at a time."

The little boy took the bottle and she grabbed a towel and put it on his chest in case he spilled. She watched him and smiled. He was their reason to continue on. They had to protect him and make sure that he didn't just survive but that he thrived. He was the reason they had to go to higher ground, he was the reason they would be alright.

"I was thinking of somewhere else that we could go, in the same area? Ideas?"

"How about George's place. You remember the contractor that built the studio and the fences for us?"

"Yea? Oh, the empty lot or lots in his subdivision?" asked Lee. He smiled and nodded at Ellen.

"Yea. If the empty lots are full of cars, maybe we can park on the street. At least for tonight? We're high enough now," said Ellen looking back over her shoulder.

"Okay."

"I also um… have a shovel if we need to dig a hole. It will be just like camping when the kids were little, won't it?" Ellen looked at him and grinned, she remembered how much he hated camping.

"Honey, I'm afraid that we're going to have to take this one day at a time and hope for the best."

She was concerned over a lot of things, would they have water, would they have electricity, would they have help from the mainland. How many people would likely die without their medication, could they get it? How many would be gone in the next three weeks, three months, six months or a year?

One Day At A Time

Ellen stopped the racing thoughts in her mind, she had to focus on what was happening right now and deal with the problems and solutions in front of them.

She knew there were people that lived off the grid here on the Sunshine Coast so if they had to face this crisis this was a good place to be. Only time would tell but right now she had to calm her mind about the what-ifs.

They reached the cross roads of the main highway and drove to the other side.

Ellen felt herself relax. They were well over the tsunami level now.

"Keep driving, I see that the Safeway is full, but I still see empty lots in George's subdivision. We're going to be okay, at least for today," Ellen said as she reached over and squeezed Lee's hand.

All they could do was do their best, and as Lee said, take it one day at a time.

Once Upon A Time

"ONCE UPON A TIME, NOT THAT LONG AGO, there was a city called Vancouver, in a province called British Columbia, in a country called Canada. This city had millions of people in it and huge buildings. The buildings were so tall the sunlight never reached the ground, everything was in shadow all day and all night."

I paused to gaze at my audience. Their mouths hung open and their eyes were round with disbelief.

My audience was three small children, one little boy, and two little girls, not one over the age of six. They started to push each other as they sat under an old blanket in front of the fire.

The others had finished their evening chores and settled in front of the fire as well. I hoped by the telling of stories and the singing of songs that some of the old information would be preserved for future generations.

"Jenna, go on," said one of the little girls as she shoved the little boy who was trying to get her attention by pulling her blonde braid.

"Yeah, Jenna, go on. By the way, what's a million?" asked my husband Grant in his deep bass voice.

I glanced at him and gave him a smile. He had a way of always making me feel good. I continued my story.

"Do you see the rocks on the hill, and the gravel we climbed to look for the salmon?" I asked the children.

The children nodded at me and smiled. I had their attention again. "Well, there are probably a million rocks there. Do you see the large skeletons of the old redwoods and cedars?" They nodded. "Well, these buildings were even higher than some of them."

I heard the crackle and pop of the dead wood in our fire and smelled the dust and dirt a short distance from the cave we used as a shelter.

I swallowed, but my mouth was so dry that my tongue stuck to the roof of it. I licked my cracked lips anyway to give them a little moisture, but I was left with the metallic taste of blood.

I watched Grant give some water to one of the children and the other two asked for some, too. I looked at him and handed him my ration.

He nodded and smiled at me as he gave them a few swallows each. It wasn't much, but it would have to do.

He returned my water flask and I took a small sip, just enough to rinse my mouth, and slowly swallowed the remaining few drop. I quickly sealed up the flask to make sure that none of the precious liquid evaporated.

We sat in front of a cave in North Vancouver. There was once a temperate rain forest here but now it was as dry as a dessert. That was before "The Event", as we called it.

We were fortunate to be living in Vancouver. When the comet hit it was one-third of the way around the world, deep in the Atlantic Ocean. It wasn't the original hit: it was the aftermath that caused the worst damage. There were storms, fires, tsunamis and flooding. The entire planet felt as if it was pitched to one side and shaken, as if a terrier that had gotten hold of a rat and was trying to snap its neck. I was certain that this half of North America was going to break off at some fault line. The entire city was leveled.

Gone were the impressive tall building with their icy glass walls. Gone were the bridges, all fallen onto the ground or into the water they spanned. The highways and sky train were just partial twisted pathways going nowhere.

All that was left were stumps of a once thriving civilization.

A large percentage of the population had died as each new and more devastating catastrophe had washed the earth clean. Until there was only a couple of handfuls of people left. At least that's all that we had encountered so far.

But as suddenly as it had started it stopped.

Then it was quiet. Not a sound. No barking dogs, no birds, no cars, no radios. Nothing.

Silence was one of the hardest things to get used to. I had always had background noise around me: the sounds of cars or airplanes, the constant hum of electricity. The quiet was deafening. Luckily I had Grant and now we had the others. The sounds of their movements helped to ease the feeling that I was completely alone.

Gone were the tall majestic evergreens and the dense forest floor covered with fern and salal. Before, the forest had been a place where there was rich spongy soil underfoot and you heard the constant bubbling of ice-cold streams and the piney taste of cool forest air was thick on the tongue and face.

Now everything was dead and dry.

We needed water.

We found shelter when we traveled from South Hill in Vancouver to the caves and canyons of North Vancouver. But we would need a better shelter, a place with water and somewhere to rebuild.

We had been hit hard in the last three months, but it seemed the situation was stabilized. We hoped.

"Lucy, would you like some help with the children?" I asked as I finished the last of the song requests and put my guitar away.

Lucy was a pretty little Chinese woman who was at the end of her pregnancy. Her belly was large and distended.

"No, I'm fine. It's the least I can do with me like this right now."

There were only twelve adults we encountered as we traveled across Vancouver. We had called out as we went and the dogs had gotten good at scenting and finding people. That's how we had found Kent, a man in his mid- twenties, a banker and Winston, the little boy. They had both been trapped in rubble, but Grant and I managed to dig them out.

In total we had three women and myself. I was past childbearing age so I knew that I wasn't as important as the other women. I also looked at my husband Grant. We were traditionalist and our vows meant a lot to each other. But that was then and this was now.

Times had changed a lot of things, but our marriage? I sighed as the hard thoughts and ideas came to me.

In the end that seemed to have been what killed most of the population being killed where they lived or trapped in the buildings not able to get out. Then it was lack of electricity, medication and sanitation. It seemed that for a long time we had one epidemic after another and only the strong and the lucky lived through it.

"Everyone, I think that we need to talk. It's time to have a meeting. Let's say in about ten minutes?" said Grant.

I almost said that most of us didn't have watches since most people used to use their cell phones to check the time, but now there wasn't any electricity, the grid was completely down, and it wouldn't be up for a very long time, if ever. But old habits were hard to break sometimes.

Lucy came back from tucking the children into their beds at the back of the cave. It was cooler there and easier to protect them from the predators that had become more and more aggressive.

We had already had run-ins with bears and had a cougar sighting. There were packs of dogs that had quickly gone feral and were getting bolder. Luckily we found rifles and handguns in the local Gold and Gun store. We had to teach each other how to shoot.

"Okay, I'm here. Let's get the show on the road," said Lucy as she carefully lowered herself onto a fallen log that we had pulled over to the side of the fire pit.

I looked at everyone and waited. We had all been talking about what we needed to do to survive.

It was late spring and warm. I wasn't sure if the planet had shifted its axis and we were going to have warmer weather. For all I knew we had been pushed closer to the sun, but I really didn't think so. I wished I had paid more attention to some of those science and discovery programs when I had the chance to.

Before the comet hit we were told that it wasn't as big as the one that had caused the dinosaurs to become extinct. But I wondered how they really knew; after all they weren't here then. It was all a guess as far as I know. These were the same people who said we should make sure that we had enough food and water for about a week or two.

Boy, were their estimates off. Or perhaps they downplayed the Event so that people wouldn't panic. People did anyway. When cars plugged up the all of the exits out of the city, they tried walking and thousands of people were caught out in the open during the worst of it.

"Okay, we need to find water," Kent said as he started the conversation.

"We need a good supply of food. The kids need milk. We have enough powdered milk from the grocery stores to last for a while, but fresh is better," said Lucy.

"I've made up a list of things that we need. It's a long list and includes everything from horses, cows, and goats to bees and chickens and nuts and seeds. And tools, we need tools too," said Grant as he pulled out a piece of paper from his dirt crusted jeans pocket.

I nodded and smiled. It was going well. Grant and I had spoken earlier about some of the things that were important to have.

"Bees, what the hell are we going to do with bees?" asked Dorothy, a woman in her early thirties. She had long brown hair the she was now wearing in a long braid. A hairstyle that most of the woman had adopted these days, myself included.

"A lot of things: They naturally will help pollinate the crops for us and will produce honey, probably our only sugar, as well as wax that we can use to make candles," said Grant.

Listening to him made me proud. He had actually listened to me when we had discussed things that I had been thinking about even before the Event.

I watched the other women, and Kent the other male.

I knew that if we were the only people that were left in this area we would need to make all the babies we could. We didn't know how the rest of the world fared, there could be pockets where others had survived, but so far it didn't look great for the human race. And the only way to improve the odds of human survival would be to have the most diverse genetic pool that we could. It was long range planning, but we had to take everything into account.

I felt bile rise up in my throat. I loved my husband, but we were in our fifties. I couldn't help by having children but he still could. I knew that he took the vows we made to each other seriously, but these were different times.

"Who knows anything about stupid bees?" asked Shirley, a teenage girl from a comfortable gated community.

"I do," I answered.

"It's not the only thing we need. But Jenna and I know a man from our old neighborhood that has the knowledge that we need. He has the farmer and woodsman stuff down pat. He even built his own bread kiln in his back yard. He heated it with wood and it worked perfectly. He grew all his own vegetables and even had a beehive. The food was fresh and delicious. This was all in the city."

I waited for them to reach the only conclusion that they could. I watched as each face reached it.

"Someone is going to have to go into the middle of the city and see what can be saved. There may be other things we can salvage in time, but I know where he lives and where the bees.

He was alive when we left, but he wanted to stay there waiting for his children hoping that they would come home."

I smoothed down my top as I stood and wrapped my shawl tightly around me. My fingers played with the short fringe at the ends and I knew that I was showing my nervousness. The dogs at my feet stood up and stretched. They looked at me waiting.

"I volunteer to go to South Hill and see what I can come back with. I'll copy the list we have and if there is anything else that we need, that we can't get close by, we'll add it to the list," I said.

I was pleased with myself; my voice was calm and steady even though the acid in my belly was tearing me apart. I looked around the dying fire and looked at everyone in turn and smiled confidently but I hadn't looked at Grant once.

I had already spoken and discussed this with Grant and Ken and they had both agreed.

Neither had been happy with the idea and Grant and I had discussed it until there weren't any more words. All we could do is love each other while we had the time to be together.

"We need you here to help us. And you can't go by yourself it's too dangerous," said Lucy looking afraid.

I looked her in the eyes and lied. "Thanks, Lucy. That's sweet of you; it's not that bad. I'll be fine. I won't be gone that long and I bet that I'll be back before that baby of your comes. Okay?"

The odds of me making it back weren't very good. We had had a really difficult time getting here in the first place.

A couple of the other females looked at each other and at Lucy. The two of us were the only women experienced in having children and they were counting on us. But they only needed one, so I was the one that should go. That might make things easier for Grant and the other women.

I kept telling myself I was being logical and making a hard decision for the best interest of the group.

"I'll be leaving as soon as possible. I'll be walking, but I would like to take Buster along with me."

Buster was a large golden retriever and would be good company on the trip.

If I was lucky and got some things that were awkward to carry, I was planning to hitch a drag carrier to him.

"You can keep Page." I said to Grant. "She's good at finding and catching rabbits so you'll have some fresh meat for the pot while I'm gone. And most importantly I can be on the lookout for water as I travel. I'll make a map and keep a journal about what I find. That way we can use the information when I get back to decide if we should go and where we should go to."

I knew I had them. I had erased any doubts about leaving our little happy group at the mention of water.

I didn't want to go, but I was the best choice, actually the only choice. I had the best chance of getting there and getting back as quickly as possible while the others took care of the hunting and fishing and protecting the camp.

I watched them as they all started to nod in agreement. We had up to now always stuck together and helped each other this was the first time our little group was splitting up and no one liked it. But we needed the information and the bees, it had to be done and they all realized it.

**

I made good time getting out of North Vancouver.

While the roads were buckled and the buildings pretty much leveled it wasn't too bad. I was getting used to it and finding ways around the worst of the destruction. It was still going to be a long journey, probably a good week.

I was lucky and soon found little ponds of ground water to keep Buster and me from becoming dehydrated. I stopped at grocery store that was not one of the ones we were using for supplies and got enough supplies for the journey.

It really was incredible how everything in the city was so much cleaner than it ever was before the Event. The air was so clear that it was almost painful to look at the horizon. You used to see just a faint outline of the Gulf Islands, but now you could see the shorelines and each island standing out from the others.

At night the sky was so clear and the moon and stars so close that you could almost touch them. The light from the stars high overhead, hung in the air like diamonds scattered on a dark blue velvet curtain. And the moon was a large pale white pearl hanging there, shining gently down on the new world. It all looked so normal, but the stars weren't really in the place that they should be, or that I remembered that they should be. The Big Dipper was there, but it was low in the horizon.

I couldn't remember if it was that way or if it should be directly overhead. We really needed books from the library another thing that we would have to do soon.

On the third day of going up Indian Arm, Buster and I found a boat that was still seaworthy and we took it across and entered Vancouver. When we landed and I pulled the boat ashore for the return trip. Buster jumped out of the boat and ran around, he stopped, stood still and lifted his muzzle into the air. He moved his head back and forth as he tested the air to locate the scent that had caught his attention.

I heard a deep guttural woof and a heavy shuffling lumbering sound that didn't belong to any dog I had ever encountered.

It was a bear; I quickly dropped my pack and got my rifle out. It was a light rifle and knew that it wouldn't do much good in this situation.

"Buster, come here. Stay," I said to the dog in a firm tone.

I knew that the best plan was to get out of the area as soon as possible. I didn't know if it was a sow with cubs or a big old male bear. I knew that their normal food wouldn't be available this year and that would be making them hungry and mean.

I picked up my pack and slung it onto my back as I tried to grab Buster.

But Buster saw the bear and started barking; the bear came around the corner of a low wrecked building and charged straight at us. It was a big male and it was mad. I looked around for the nearest building that would give us shelter. It was across a wide expanse of road and rock. I knew we wouldn't make it, but had to try.

I steadied the rifle and quickly fired off two shots and yelled and screamed as loud as I could as I ran toward the bear waving my arms. Then I stopped and ran the other way still screaming and waving my arms over head.

My idea of shock and awe didn't work and the bear didn't turn away. Instead he stood up on his hind legs and roared and he swiped his lethal front paws at us.

"Come on, Buster, run!" I yelled at him as I led the way across the road.

He didn't follow me.

I heard a combination of roaring from the bear and frenzied barking and growling from Buster.

I glanced over my shoulder as I ran. Buster was playing a dangerous game with the bear. He ducked between the bear's paws, snapped his teeth and then ran away. He managed it a few times and then I heard a loud horrible yelping and a howl of pain.

I got to the building, stopped and turned to look at Buster and raised my rifle. I couldn't shoot; the bear had him against his chest between his front paws. Then I saw it drop Buster, lift a paw and rake its claws down Buster. I watched him go limp, his head hanging to one side and I knew that he was dead.

The bear picked him up, shook Buster again, dropped him then turned and headed toward Burnaby.

Buster had saved me. Tears filled my eyes and I started to sob. I leaned against the building and swallowed hard trying to catch my breath. I couldn't believe that Buster was dead. It happened so quickly. He was a brave dog; a good dog and I would miss him. I started to cry again, and rubbed my eyes hard with my hand.

I was all alone.

I had no one to even talk too, but I couldn't stop. I knew that people were waiting for me and I had to press on. If this mission were to be successful I would have to keep going while there was daylight. I started walking again.

The following day, the fifth, I got to Knight Road and followed it all the way to South Hill and to my old home. It was so strange walking in the old neighborhood a place that was so familiar and now looked so different.

The worst was the smell. The sewage system must have broken and there was no one to take care of the bodies of the people and their pets.

I heard the yowl of feral cats and saw a small pack of midsized dogs, but they stayed away from me. I knew that I had to be very careful. Individually they were fine, but as a pack they could easily take down and kill a person.

I looked up and saw smoke coming from the back of old man Kurt's place and I smiled. My trip was not a waste. Now all I had to do was to convince him to come with me.

His knowledge and experience in the old ways of growing crops and taking care of animals could mean the difference between our survival and the extinction of the human race. I felt that with him we had a chance, a good chance.

I went around the side of the house and stepped over the fallen wooden fence that used to separate his property from his neighbor's. There was no one there anymore so it wasn't needed.

"Kurt, it's Jenna, your neighbor from across the street."

I waited. There was no sound, no answer.

"Kurt. Are you home?" I called again.

"Ya. Come on," said a weak trembling voice.

I heard the bark of a dog as I came around the corner of the ruined house. There was a tan shepherd looking warily at me. It's barking became frenzied. I froze.

"Kurt. You got yourself a dog?"

He had never had the time for dogs, preferring cats as company.

"Lucky. Enough," said Kurt.

The dog quieted and I moved forward.

I found Kurt. He was lying on a sleeping bag under a tarp that he had strung between four tall logs. It looked kind of like a teepee. He looked very old and grey. His eyes were sunken and bloodshot.

I was shocked and upset at the change in him, but I knew that I couldn't let it show. We really needed him.

"What happened, Kurt?" I asked as I knelt down beside him.

"Well, it's like I say. You never know, do you?"

I leaned over and felt his forehead. He didn't have a fever.

"No, it's my heart. No more medicine," he said.

"I'm waiting for the kids. They should be home soon," he mumbled to himself. "Everything's gone. They're all dead, you know."

"Kurt, I'm going to make you some tea from foxglove. Okay? We'll try it weak first."

"I don't have any."

"No, but I do in my old yard and so do the neighbors. I saw it as I was coming here. How are you fixed for water?"

"Got plenty in the garage."

I busied myself and got some of the plant leaves from next door and a fire going in his fire pit. I filled the cast iron pot he had on a three-legged iron stand and left it to boil. Then I pulled a cushion from the swinging couch and put it next to the fire so I could keep and eye on Kurt.

Lucky settled down and soon she was following me around. I took a quick look to see what he had growing. After the foxglove tea, I knew that I could make a nice vegetable soup with the fresh tomatoes, beans and garlic chives he had growing. He even had a small patch of corn and I pulled a couple of ears off to roast on the fire.

"Kurt, we need your help. We need to find water and learn about bees and growing crops. There are about a dozen of us in the foothills of North Vancouver," I swallowed hard. "We can start again, but it would be easier if we had help."

During the next few days I watched him and waited.

During these times I've seen amazing things and sometimes people will rally if they have a reason for going on. But it didn't happen. I was surprised; I would never have thought that Kurt would give up. Maybe his heart couldn't be helped with the simple tea we had.

I needed to make him realize how important he is to us.

"We'll take our time and you'll get stronger."

He looked me in the eyes and shook his head.

"Listen. You'll be fine. I have books. Take them, but please leave a note for the kids. They'll be home soon." His voice drifted off.

Me? Who was he kidding? I didn't know anything, not like he did. He had the knowledge and the practical experience. He was the valuable one.

I slowly realized that if Kurt was valuable with his old knowledge, maybe I was too? There wasn't anyone else but me to pass on the survival knowledge.

The thought terrified me.

I knew that I couldn't do it alone. I took a deep breath and felt a calmness and strength come over me.

A short while later he patted my hand as his eyes slowly closed and one last long sigh escaped from his lips.

I knew he was gone.

I cried for a long time. He was a good man and I didn't know what to do. It would take me hours to bury him and it seemed almost pointless with all the other dead in the city, but I didn't want the animals to get him.

I walked over to the beehive that he kept by the side of the garage with its partially caved in roof and looked at it. It was quiet. I waited for a few minutes to see if any bees would come out or go in. Not a bee in sight at the hive.

I had really hoped that Kurt would be able to help us. I didn't know what to do now. Grant and I were the oldest people in our group and we had very little experience with raising vegetables or fruit. But Kurt was a wise man and he seemed to think that I could do it. I would have to give it my all and I would.

I looked around the yard and found a long cement structure that was low to the ground. It was about four feet high and had a cement floor with an area for drainage. I realized that this must be the start of a new building or experiment that Kurt was doing, but I saw that this would be a perfect place for his body. I could use some of the metal roofing that had fallen down from his garage for its roof and then I could weigh it down with some heavy rubble to keep out the animals.

It took a while to get everything ready, but finally I went back to get Kurt's body. When I was finished I said a few words and a small prayer. I knew he would have liked that.

I was tired, very tired, bone tired. I sat down in the shade of the garage. Lucky came and sat a short distance from me and watched me. Books. Kurt said he had books. I knew that he would also have seeds that would help. I wouldn't be going home empty handed.

I slept for a long time. It was a very deep and restful sleep. As I woke I stretched my whole body from my fingers to my toes, it felt good.

The sun was warm on my face and a gentle breeze tickled my face. It was so relaxing with the sun, the breeze, and the drone of bees in the background. It was a lovely morning.

My eyes snapped open and I made sure that I didn't move.

Bees. I saw one slowly fly by me. Okay, they were bees, but were they the right kind? I got up and followed the little fellow to a small hive, about the size of a grapefruit between the branches of a tree a short distance from the old hive.

I carefully looked at the bees coming from the hive and then went to the old hive. They certainly looked the same.

I knew that if the old queen died the hive would move with a new queen. These bees had the same markings as the dead ones around the old hive so I knew that it was worth the risk and trouble of moving them.

Kurt had a small light, wide wooden cart in the back of the yard and I had seen that it was still there and seemed unharmed.

I emptied out the old hive of the little bodies, but kept the honeycomb. I hoped that the heat and lack of water when the comet hit had killed them, not some pre-Event virus.

I got the cart pulled up to the old hive and loaded it. I went to Kurt's green house that was covered with a light clear plastic tarp and looked in his garage and workshop. He had cleaned up and repaired a lot of the damage. I found books on topics that wouldn't be in modern libraries or bookstores.

I smiled to myself. These were books with basic old-time knowledge, written simply, beautifully illustrated and easy to follow.

I found a length of rope and managed to leash Lucky to the cart. She didn't take much persuading after I gave her a drink of water and some food. She was a docile female and a nice little girl despite the earlier growls.

I was very pleased to have a new companion and protector.

I wasn't sure how to move the little hive. Then I remembered that Kurt had bees shipped to him once in a small wooden box about the size of the old style matchboxes. I needed to find something that would let the air in, but would keep the bees contained.

I carefully went up the back stairs into the remains of the house. One side had completely collapsed, but the other side that had the chimney and the stairs to the basement and the second floor was still standing. I found a piece of cheesecloth in the basement that I hoped would do the trick.

Kurt's house had held up better than most of its neighbors after the earthquakes and fires.

The fire ravaged some area and left others untouched. Some blocks were completed blackened and flattened and others not so bad. A few small areas had a house or two that you might be able to live in, but there was nothing around and no sewage or electricity.

I loaded everything I could find that would be of use and would fit into the small cart. Lucky and I headed out the next morning at first light. I left a couple of notes for Kurt's children. That way if they ever did come home they would be able to find us.

There was still a lot at Kurt's place that we could use and a lot of information in the old-fashioned books I had to leave behind, but I could only take so much with me. When I got back, the group would have to decide whether or not someone should make this dangerous trip again. We would make that decision together.

I was pleased with what I was coming back with, but it didn't really solve the problem of water. We needed a sustainable water supply.

***

I entered the area below our cave site and looked up at the mountains. It did feel like I was coming home. It was amazing that in the few months after the Event sprigs of green were starting to break though the ground.

Fireweed. That's what would grow first and then other plants would follow. Good old mother earth would be fine.

It was getting to be dusk. I stopped to watch the western sky turn from the bight blue of the day to pink and purple. Were those wisps of cloud? Might the rain return?

I heard the children before I saw them and they came scrambling toward me asking for a story. I laughed at their excitement.

Then came Grant, with his arms wide open.

He held me close and kissed me hard. I felt like my heart was going to break. I knew that I would have to make sure he did what we needed for the survival of people.

"I've missed you so much," he said through his tears. "Who do you have with you?" he asked to distract me as he looked at the dog.

Kent came up and gave me a quick hug too and took the cart.

"This is Lucky. She was with Kurt. He's dead. Buster died too. But I got bees, a hive, a whole bunch of seeds and books on all different topics. I'll tell you all about it," I said as we walked the rest of the way to camp.

"Good, you did really well. I was worried."

I nodded. I didn't really know what to say to him.

I walked into the camp and quickly kissed and hugged everyone. Then they left us alone so that we could have some time to ourselves.

We walked past the cave to a small flat rock. We sat in silence, just holding hands and looking at each other until it was so dark we couldn't see anymore.

"I've been thinking," he said.

I waited for him. I knew that this was going to be an important talk.

"I want you to trust me and I want to talk to you about two things. One is water. Do you remember the old stories Kurt used to tell, about his father finding water for the neighbors and how he did it a couple of times too?" Grant slipped a forked shaped tree branch into my hands. "I think it's willow, but I'm not sure."

"Oh, come on," I started to say and then stopped. I felt a strange light pull toward the ground when I slipped both my hands on the short sections of the branch. Strange, I'll have to take a closer look at it tomorrow it was worth further exploration. But not today, not when I could relax in Grant's arms for the first time in two weeks.

I could tell from his eyes that he was serious.

"The second is more important. You and me, I've been giving it a lot of thought and I think that I can help out and "do my duty" as they say, but still keep our commitment to each other. I think that we can accomplish both if we use some modern conveniences."

Now I noticed a bright glint in his eyes and a smile trying to break free around his mouth and he pulled out a turkey baster and handed it to me.

I looked at him speechless.

"You tell me that artificial insemination works really well for the birds and the bees. Well how about people? I know it's been done."

I started to laugh.

I knew that he was serious, but it was so ridiculous. It was also worth a try, both that and the dowsing were worth a try.

Just then I heard three little voices chanting louder and louder.

"Once upon a time. Once upon a time."

I knew that I was being called and I had to answer.

Grant and I went to the fire pit and found comfortable seats.

I began my story for the evening.

"Once upon a time there was a man named Kurt..."

Countdown

ELVIS PEPPER SAT ON HIS BUNK staring at the image on the monitor on his desk. His eyes brimmed with tears and his mind was having trouble processing what he was seeing.

When the asteroid the size of Texas struck the Earth in the Atlantic Ocean it vaporized that ocean and hurled a huge cloud of dust and debris high into the atmosphere. The clouds of superheated air quickly formed a shroud around the Earth and winds spread a wave of destruction at speeds of over two hundred and fifty miles an hour outward in waves from the epicenter where the asteroid struck.

The surveillance satellite watching the catastrophe was stationed within range of the electromagnetic pulse so as expected within a few minutes of impact the satellite's transmission feed was lost.

As the screen changed to white fuzz a tear escaped Elvis' right eye and travelled down his cheek. In the next few hours everything humanity had built over the last ten thousand years would be scoured from the surface of the planet by a force greater than the collective power of every atomic weapon ever constructed. Nature had provided a far more lethal end for the Earth than mankind ever could.

The four orbiting Lagrange stations in Earth orbit, and the fifth at L2 position on the other side of the moon, would keep the dream of humanity alive. All that remained now of the human race were twenty thousand Adam and Eve's to start over, and hopefully some day re-populate the Earth.

Like a zombie Elvis got up from his bunk and walked to the desk where he fingered the off button on the side of the monitor and it went dark. He let out a slow breath. He'd been preparing for this day for five years yet when the time came the image of such terrible destruction affected him at a far deeper level than he had anticipated.

After he wiped his eyes with the back of his hand then went to the door of his cabin and keyed the code into the keypad in the wall next to the door. There was a barely audible click before the door side aside and he stepped into the corridor.

Countdown

He passed several cabin doors on his way to the communication center where he was due to relieve Selma Hollings. It had been two hours since impact and they were supposed to keep monitoring communications from the underground bunkers where other survivors were housed, and the other L stations.

The bunkers were constructed in the twentieth century during the cold war, and now in the middle of the twenty-first century the bunkers were being used to protect a cadre of scientists and other experts that were unsuccessful in the world wide lottery for the twenty thousand coveted positions on the Lagrangian stations, or those deemed ineligible for the lottery due to age or for medical reasons but were still valuable.

Only fertile people between the ages of twelve and forty-five were eligible to enter the lottery, but the worlds leading scientists agreed these bunkers would save an additional thirty thousand people. They expected these survivors would be able to hold out in the bunkers for the next five years. Estimates were until the dust and debris thrown into the atmosphere would have settled by then.

But Elvis wasn't worried about the survival of thirty thousand people. He was concerned about the survival of one person. His wife Yvette.

Her PhD in immunization technology made her eligible for the bunker in the Ural Mountains after she was deemed unsuitable for the lottery. Her inability to have children made her ineligible to even apply. But her scientific expertise made her indispensible for the future survival in the harsh environment expected in five years.

He told her wouldn't go without her, but he would never have qualified for one of the bunkers. After many long, tearful arguments he agreed to go to the L1 station. They would stay linked by com sat as long as they were able. They would both survive just not together.

Now that he'd witnessed the destruction he knew he'd made the wrong decision.

I should have stayed with her as long as possible, he thought. But then I'd be dead.

A lump of fear knotted his guts and his heart beat hard in his chest. He grew more anxious with each step as he raced to the communications center. He was one of five specialists responsible to maintain and operate the com systems between the stations. And for the time being with any Earth based survivors.

The stations were shielded against electromagnetic interference so unlike the satellites they would be able to maintain communications.

"I need to stay focused," he muttered as he passed cabin after cabin. The sobs his fellow survivors echoed in the empty corridor and followed him as he rushed along the corridor toward the lift that would take him to the command deck. The captain would need him today so he had to shake off his fear and his uncertainty.

Problem was he wasn't sure he could put aside what remained of his humanity. In fact he wasn't sure any of them could.

The lift doors closed behind him after he entered. Good thing he was alone because he wanted to scream out how unfair all this was. He closed his eyes and sighed.

The end of the world, the separation from his wife, the end of everything he held dear felt like a tremendous weight crushing him under with despair.

He would never feel a warm breeze on his face or witness the sunrise over the purple mountains of his late father's cabin on Seesaw Mountain. He'd never swim in the ocean or smell wood smoke from a campfire.

Stars would never twinkle again and his dog would never run in the tall grass behind his uncle's barn.

The doors opened as the lift stopped on the command deck. He opened his eyes and stepped out just before the doors closed behind him.

No one was around, he was alone. He walked to the com panel and touched the power button. The board lit up and the screens came to life. Even though the station was shielded the captain ordered all nonessential systems be powered down until after impact.

The screens flickered then steadied. The external cameras directed at Earth showed the fierce red cloud of energy had spread half way across the United States laying waste to cities, towns, open plains, everything. Every plant, animal and human would be vaporized. No pain, no suffering.

In a way he almost envied them. At least their end would be quick. If the eggheads were correct the debris trailing the asteroid might end this attempt at keeping the human race viable might even before it began. A rocky missile the size of a tennis ball would puncture the station and compromise its atmosphere killing most if not all of the inhabitants in the process.

Countdown

Elvis felt smaller and more insignificant than he had ever in his life. "Activate holo-assistant," he said as he picked up a com node and placed it in his right ear.

There was a shimmer and Maple appeared next to him. She wore a sad-eyed, sympathetic expression on her holographic features. Dressed in her lab suit and with the glasses perched on the end of her small nose she looked every part the scientist the designer had built into her.

Though Elvis knew her emotions were memory engrams programmed into her matrix he really needed a friend right now. Since Maple had been with him since his training started five years ago she had become just a friend. He smiled to himself as he recalled the memory of Yvette actually getting jealous of the "other woman" in his life.

"Good times," he said quietly.

"I disagree," said Maple in a dulcet tone.

Elvis paused to look at her. "What?"

"Well, sir this is not a *good time*, as you put it. It is the end of planet Earth as a home for humans."

"Thanks for reminding me," he said sarcastically. He shook his head. "I was recalling one happy memory and you had to ruin it."

Maple's eyes widened. "Sorry, sir. Sometimes I forget my manners."

"Never mind. Contact L3 and see if they can get me an angle of the bunker in the Ural Mountains. Or is that too difficult?"

"No, sir right away."

There was a short pause and a familiar voice came through the com node in his ear. "L3, Pumper Jackson speaking'."

"Pump, it's E. I need a link to your cams directed at the Ural bunkers."

"Hey, E. Man, wasn't that impact thingy sumthin?"

"Yeah, Pump it was that." His heart skipped a beat and for a second he thought his next words would catch in his throat. He coughed then managed to say, "Anyway, can you set up the link?"

"Isn't that where Yvette is?"

'Yeah, Pump she's there. And will you boost the signal for me so I can talk to her?"

"I need authorization from —"

"Really, Pump? Really?! It's me, Pump!" He tried to control the anger in his voice but failed. He didn't need a lecture on procedure right now. He needed to talk to his wife before it was too late.

Elvis sighed heavily and his shoulders slumped. "Sorry, Pump. I didn't mean to be short with you. It's just that —" His next words caught at the back of his throat.

"Yeah, okay, E. No problemo. I'll have Lucy establish the link right away." Lucy was Pump's holo-assistant. "Set your monitor to receive."

"It's done, sir," Maple said before he issued the order.

The monitor flickered then steadied and he could see the Ural range untouched, pristine and rugged jutting into the sky.

West of the mountains the edge of the shock wave headed across Europe. It had just wiped away Germany. Millions of people died as he stared at the monitor.

He swallowed hard then said, "L1 to Ural Command, over."

Silence.

"L1 to Ural command," he repeated.

There was a crackle of static then a heavily accented voice responded. "This is Ural Command. Ivan the Terrible speaking. Go ahead L1."

"Ivan!" Elvis smiled to himself. The big man had befriended both he and Yvette during the initial training phase.

They had enjoyed dinners and golf games with Ivan and his wife, Simone. Simone won a spot of L2 so Ivan and he had that much in common. "How're things going?"

"EP! How nice to hear your voice, my friend. So far everything is going as planned. We lost contact with the Washington bunkers and the ones in Berlin, Helsinki and Ottawa but they told us that would happen. We're anticipating to reestablish contact twelve hours after the impact wave has dissipated." There was a brief pause. "According to current estimates that should be in two days."

Elvis swiveled in his seat to face Maple. He removed the com node from his ear and wrapped it tight in his fist. He motioned for the hologram to lean closer. "How long until the impact wave reaches the Urals?" he whispered.

"Seventeen minutes," she said.

He nodded then placed the node back in his ear and turned back to face the monitor. "Ivan, I need to speak with Yvette. Can you patch me through?"

"Yes, of course."

There was another pause then his wife's voice came over the node. "E?" she said. He could hear the fear in her voice.

Elvis swallowed hard as his mouth dried. "You okay, my love?"

"Yes. So far," came the reply.

"So far?"

"There have been fifteen suicides reported in the past hour."

No! She couldn't. There was still a chance however small. "How about you?" His voice trembled as he spoke and his heart began to beat faster.

"Don't be concerned, E. Suicide has never been part of my make up."

He heard her swallow and wanted to jump through the com system to wrap her in his arms. "I know, Yvette. It's just up until now this nightmare has been theoretical. The reality is very different. I'm worried what any of us will do."

"Did you see the impact?" she said changing the subject.

"Yes," he whispered. As long as he lived he'd never forget what he'd seen. That terrible image had been burned into his brain permanently.

"The captain has ordered a full briefing in ten minutes," interrupted Maple. "He wants the entire population to meet in the recreation hall."

He looked at Maple and raised both eyebrows. She understood his meaning.

They were on a countdown.

"Fourteen minutes," she said softly.

"Advise my section chief I'll be late."

"I don't think—" Elvis silenced the hologram with a glare.

"Yes, sir."

Elvis flushed the sudden burst of anger from his system by rolling his shoulders and expelling a long, deep breath.

"E, are you okay?" asked Yvette.

"Yes, of course. Don't be concerned about me. I'll be right here after the impact wave has passed your bunker. And I'm staying at this post until we reestablish contact. Nothing or no one can budge me. Like I told you when we last saw each other we will never be apart, ever."

"But they could charge you with something. Maybe treason, or worse."

Yvette had always been too sweet for her own good. It was why he loved her so much. But what did any of that matter now? The governments and their laws that had ruled the planet had been swept away like so many dry leaves in the fall. The chances of any of them, or their eventual offspring, surviving were a long shot and they all knew it. Slim as the odds were they had to at least try.

The struggle for survival was what made them human.

"Yvette, my darling does any of that matter anymore?"

She laughed half-heartedly. "No, I guess not."

Elvis glanced at Maple. She held up two fingers. Two minutes until contact. He was running out of time.

"Yvette, I want you to know I don't blame you for us not being able to have children. The lab accident wasn't your fault. I never thought that not for one millisecond."

"It's okay, E," she said. "You're just—" A sudden burst of static ion his ear forced him to pull the com node from his ear. He looked at Maple and she nodded and averted her eyes. The wave of superheated air had struck the Ural mountain range knocking out all communications.

His heart racing Elvis stuffed the com node back in his ear as his eyes flitted over the monitors. The one directed at the Urals showed a blistering mass of red, orange and blue clouds engulfing the entire thousand-mile mountain range. He imagined the iron and minerals in those mountains turning to liquid. Peaks thousands of feet high were melting like molten lead.

How anyone would survive the inferno he didn't know, but his wife had to survive. She just had to.

"Sir?" said Maple from behind him.

"Yes, Maple what is it?"

"Sir, we have to go to the briefing. The signal alarm has been sounding for the last five minutes."

"Yes, of course." He decided to make a call before he left the com room. "L1 to L3."

"Go ahead, EP I've been monitoring the situation. What can I do?"

Good old, Pump, he thought, always watching my back. "Thanks, Pump. Keep watch over the Urals and let me know when the cloud clears and when you receive a signal. Okay?"

"No worries, 'ol buddy. You'll be the first to know when I hear the first peep."

"I'll call you later."

"Roger that. L3 out."

Elvis took out the node and put it back in the sterile holder he'd taken it from and stood. He glanced down at the monitor. The boiling terrible clouds rolled steadily east across the Russian steppes toward it's opposite number coming from the west.

Countdown

It appeared the two clouds of destruction would meet over Japan and together burn those islands off the map.

Elvis sighed then headed for the door to the corridor and the lift. The meeting better not take long. He wanted to get back here as soon as possible.

***

Elvis arrived back in the communications center alone. The briefing had lasted for two hours. He slumped down into the empty chair and leaned forward and rested his elbows on the consol. He closed his eyes. He wanted to cry but he was dry and numb from the pain of loss.

Sixty people on L1 had committed suicide after they witnessed the devastation. No one believed they'd kill themselves when the psychologists told them there would be suicides after impact. But he wasn't one of them. He agreed with the captain.

There was still hope that some of them would survive to carry on the human race.

While it was still early the news wasn't all bad.

None of the bunkers had yet made contact. And L2 hadn't checked in yet.

But in addition to their station, L3, 4 and 5 were safe and the smaller asteroids following the planet killer hadn't yet been detected anywhere near the LaGrange orbits.

Elvis made a mental note when he got through to the Urals he'd ask Ivan if he'd heard from Simone on L2. He needed to stay optimistic.

The gardens and farms on the stations and the water and air purification systems made the LaGrange stations completely self-sufficient. They could survive and in twenty or thirty years they might even be able to join the survivors on the Earth to begin rebuilding civilization. At least that was the plan.

He wondered now if it was worth it for him. The chances Yvette survived the destruction in the Urals was slim. Even though it was unlikely he'd ever see her in person again any glimmer of hope that she lived was all he had to hold onto right now.

Just as he placed the com node in his ear the screen to his left blurred then steadied. It was the feed from L3 still focused on the Urals. His heart seemed to skip a beat and he gasped when he saw the blink of bright red lights from beneath the clouds still obscuring the mountain range.

"L1 to L3. Come in, Pumper! Please come in!"

He realized he was shouting but his excitement had bubbled over.

"Yeah, E I'm here. But don't scream at me, pal. What's up?"

"Did you see that?"

"What?"

Elvis edged forward in his chair and looked hard at the monitor. The light had disappeared there were only clouds now. "Uuh, I saw a light. A red flashing light."

"I don't see anything," said Pumper. "Let me run back the recording."

The cameras images were recorded in a protein based memory storage system containing 150 billion yottabytes of information. This memory capacity had been installed in each station so the collective knowledge of mankind would remain intact for ten million years.

"Yes, you're right. There it is. Interesting."

Elvis wanted to jump through the consol his impatience threatened to overwhelm him. "Well, what do you think?"

"Let me check. Give me a few seconds."

Silence. Elvis blinked away beads of sweat that trickled into his eyes and he fidgeted in his chair as if it had suddenly become uncomfortable.

Since the chair automatically formed to the contours of the person sitting it this was impossible, but he could barely contain his nerves. Yvette could be alive somewhere down there and someone could be trying to signal them.

"Hummm, E my holo interface tells me this is a signal. A signal of human origin."

"What does it say?" Elvis blurted.

'Well, it's in Morse code..." Pumper's voice trailed off.

"Never mind all that. Is it from my wife?"

"Huh, no, E. It's an automated signal the computer was programmed to look for if the bunker..." Again his voice trailed off.

"You mean the message was to be sent if the bunker survived?"

"Huh, no. The opposite I'm afraid." Pumper paused. "I'm so sorry, E," he said his voice a whisper.

Elvis' shoulders slumped and a wave of grief washed over him in waves. She was dead. It was over. "Thanks, Pump."

He signed off and asked Maple to signal his shift replacement to take over for him. She did as he asked without question.

"I'll be in my cabin," he said before leaving the communications center.

Elvis arrived back in his cabin and sat down heavily on the bunk. He wondered what he'd do now. How would he carry on without the knowledge his beloved Yvette was alive and well? He shook his head and waited for the tears that would never come. He'd shed enough tears today.

He looked up and saw the monitor on the desk flash that a message was waiting for him. He didn't want to talk to anyone right now. All he needed was to be alone with his thoughts and his memories. It was all he had left.

He shrugged. There was no harm in checking the message. Whoever it was would have to wait for a reply but he could at least listen.

"Play message," he whispered.

The screen came to life and his eyes grew wide. It was Yvette.

"Hi, E. It's me. I left this message for you a month ago when I was told the chances of survival were less than five percent." She paused and her watery, sky-blue eyes drifted to her right away from the camera then abruptly directly into the screen. It was as if she were looking right into his heart.

Elvis swallowed the bile that had risen to the back of his throat and let a breath slowly escape from between his dry lips.

His hands trembled and a knot formed in his stomach. She looked so beautiful, so vulnerable.

"I love you, E. I always have and if there is another world beyond this one then I will wait for you as long as it takes. But I want you to do something for me. I want you to stay alive and help others to stay alive."

She paused again and her lips trembled. "And I want you to donate sperm to help the human race survive.

"I'm asking to do this because if you and other the men and women who survive don't do this then the human race's very existence will have been for nothing. I don't believe that and I know you don't believe it either.

"Please, Elvis, please promise me you'll do this. Please. And always remember, I love you."

The screen went dark.

He started when there was a knock on his door. He wiped the back of his hand across his eyes stood and walked to the door. He tapped the keypad next to the door.

The cabin door slid aside to reveal Maple standing in the corridor. Her brown eyes were slightly sad. He knew it wasn't real emotion but he appreciated the effort anyway.

"Yes, Maple what is it?"

"We just received word that L2 was damaged in a meteor shower, but they have managed to effect repairs and made contact a few minutes ago. No reported injuries."

Elvis nodded. "That is good news. Thanks, M."

The hologram nodded. "Yes, sir. I thought you'd like to know right away."

Elvis smiled at Maple then tapped the keypad next to the door and it closed.

Elvis walked to the desk where the monitor sat and sat on the chair facing the monitor. He stared at the screen.

Yes, he decided he'd do what Yvette wanted. She was right. He had a responsibility to humankind far greater than himself.

And he'd do it for Yvette.

Acknowledgements

These collections would be impossible without the skills of the artists who create the wonderful cover art, the software designers whose vision make modern publishing possible.

Thanks you to all who knowingly or unknowingly contributed to this collection.

About the Authors

Rita Schulz lives in Vancouver, B.C. with Russ, her husband who is also a fiction writer.

She loves to read and paint in her spare time. She is learning to enjoy golf, and he is learning to enjoy gardening. They are kept company, and on track, by their two dogs and Glenn, their younger son.

She has written for years and is an alumni of the Oregon Writers Network and the Greater Vancouver Chapter, Romance Writers of America. To find out more about her and her work visit her website at http://www.ritacrossley.com

International selling author, Russ Crossley, writes science fiction and fantasy, and mystery/suspense. Over his more than 15 year career he has published 10 novels and almost 100 short stories.

His latest science fiction satire set in the far future, *Revenge of the Lushites*, is a sequel to *Attack of the Lushites* released in 2011. The latest title in the series was released in the fall of 2013. Both titles are available in e-book and trade paperback.

He has sold several short stories that have appeared in anthologies from various publishers including; WMG Publishing, Pocket Books, and St. Martins Press.

He is a member of SF Canada and is past president of the Greater Vancouver Chapter of Romance Writers of America. He is also an alumni of the Oregon Coast Professional Fiction Writers Master Class taught by award winning author/editors, Kristine Katherine Rusch and Dean Wesley Smith.

Feel free to contact him on Facebook, Twitter, or his website http://www.russcrossley.com. He loves to hear from readers

Other collections of short fiction by the authors

Tales of Urban Fantasy
Five Tales of Bizarre Detectives
Tales of Mystery and Suspense
Tales of Weird Fantasy
Spies, Detectives, & Heroes
Tales of Twisted Crime
Tales of The Unexpected
Tales From Space
10 by Russ Crossley
Round Up At The Burger Bar: The Story of Trixie Pug,
Parts 1- 5 The Beginning
Worlds of Science Fiction and Fantasy
More Tales of Mystery and Suspense
Ladies of the Jolly Roger
Justice Served
Love Stories
Ladies of the Jolly Roger with Rita Schulz
The Adventures of Razor and Edge:
Five Tales From The Quirky Detective Team
An Unexpected Journey
On Edge
Thrilling Adventures
Total War
Nightmares
Ladies of the Jolly Roger
Ten Tempting Tales

The Fantastic Five
Unique Tales of the Fantastic
Tales of the Fantastic

Coming soon from
53rd Street Publishing

Nightmares come in many forms and from many places.

Blood thirsty vampires.
Flesh ripping werewolves.

Brain eating zombies.
Spirits of the dead who walk among us.
Monsters of unspeakable horror appearing from the darkness.

They attack us from the past.
They attack us from alternate realities,
They appear from the depths of unspeakable darkness thirsting on our fear.

These tales of terror are guaranteed to keep you awake at night with the lights on. So sit back keep the lights burning brightly and hope there